This igloo book belongs to:

....

Contents

igloobooks

Published in 2015
by Igloo Books Ltd, Cottage Farm, Sywell, NN6 0BJ
www.igloobooks.com

Illustrated by Gina Maldonado. Additional colour by Diane Kolar and Sophie Hanton
Written by Melanie Joyce

Cover designed by Vici Watson
Interiors designed by Kerri-Ann Hulme
Edited by Stephanie Moss

LEO002 1115
2 4 6 8 10 9 7 5 3 1
ISBN 978-1-78557-044-5

Printed and manufactured in China

Stories for 1 Year Olds

igloobooks

Bunny Fun

I bounce.

4

YOU...

bounce.

8

bounce.

They...

...bou

n C e.

Everyone bounces.

All bouncing bunnies together!

13

Tickle Time

Mummy tickles...

... tummy.

Daddy...

... tickles...

... toes.

Archie **tickles** ears.

Elsa...

...tickles
nose.

19

I tickle puppy.

Kitty...

... tickles me.

21

We're a **very**...

... **tickly** *family!*

Little Bud

Here's the sun.

Here's a...

... bud.

Split, splat... ...rain.

Thud,

thud,

thud.

27

Water trickles down below.

Then the

wind

begins to BLOW.

29

Little bud...

... opens wide.

30

Out come petals...

...tucked inside.

Look, it's the **SUN!**

Here comes a...

... shower.

33

Now Little Bud is a...

... flower!

Here's your **bowl**...

... open **Wide!**

Pop the **Sticky** spoon inside.

Soft and **Squidgy,** yum, yum, **yum.**

Lots of
food...

... inside
your tum.

Here's some...

...milk.

Tip it up.

Drink it from your little cup.

All full now, one last...

... slurp!

Pat your back and then a...

...BURP!

43

A little rest after your tea.

Cuddles as you...

...Smile at me.

Rock you **Slowly**...

... here we go.

Not too **fast...**

... and not too **slow.**

47

You're so tired. Time for bed.
Settle down,
my sleepyhead.